D1219107

Short Tales
NATIVE AMERICAN MYTHS

COYOTE, IKTOME, AND THE ROCK

A SIOUX TRICKSTER MYTH

Adapted by Anita Yasuda
Illustrated Estudio Haus

magic
wagon

visit us at www.abdopublishing.com

Published by Magic Wagon, a division of the ABDO Group, PO Box 398166, Minneapolis, MN 55439. Copyright © 2013 by Abdo Consulting Group, Inc. International copyrights reserved in all countries. All rights reserved. No part of this book may be reproduced in any form without written permission from the publisher.

Short Tales™ is a trademark and logo of Magic Wagon.

Printed in the United States of America, North Mankato, Minnesota.
052012
092012

 THIS BOOK CONTAINS AT LEAST 10% RECYCLED MATERIALS.

Adapted text by Anita Yasuda
Illustrations by Estudio Haus
Edited by Rebecca Felix
Series design by Craig Hinton

Design elements: Diana Walters/iStockphoto

Library of Congress Cataloging-in-Publication Data
Yasuda, Anita.
  Coyote, iktome, and the rock : a Sioux trickster myth / by Anita Yasuda ; illustrated by Estudio Haus.
    p. cm. -- (Short tales Native American myths)
  ISBN 978-1-61641-880-9
1. Dakota Indians--Folklore. 2. Coyote (Legendary character) 3. Iktomi (Legendary character) I. Estudio Haus (Firm) II. Title.
  E99.D1Y37 2012
  398.2089'975243--dc23
                            2012004689

MYTHICAL CHARACTERS

COYOTE
A trickster able to come back to life

IKTOME
The spider trickster who can take any form

IYA
A destructive and powerful spirit in the form of a rock

RANCHER
A man traveling home

INTRODUCTION

This legend comes from the Sioux people. The Sioux originally lived in the present-day US states of Montana, North Dakota, and South Dakota and the Canadian provinces of Alberta and Saskatchewan. The Sioux are made up of the Dakota, Lakota, and Nakota people throughout these areas.

Sioux legends are an important way for customs and histories to be passed down. The legends reflect the Sioux's respect for animals and the outdoors. Animals play an important role because of the Sioux belief that all living creatures have a spirit.

Coyote, Iktome, and the Rock comes from a retelling by Lakota elder Jenny Leading Cloud at the Rosebud Indian Reservation near White River, South Dakota, in 1967. The legend teaches people to be generous and advises that once something is given, it should never be taken back.

Long ago, Coyote had a good friend called Iktome. One day, the two friends were out for a walk when they came across a rock.

This was not an ordinary rock. The rock was called Iya. It was very special.

Beautiful green moss covered the rock in long, spidery lines. The mossy lines had a story to tell.

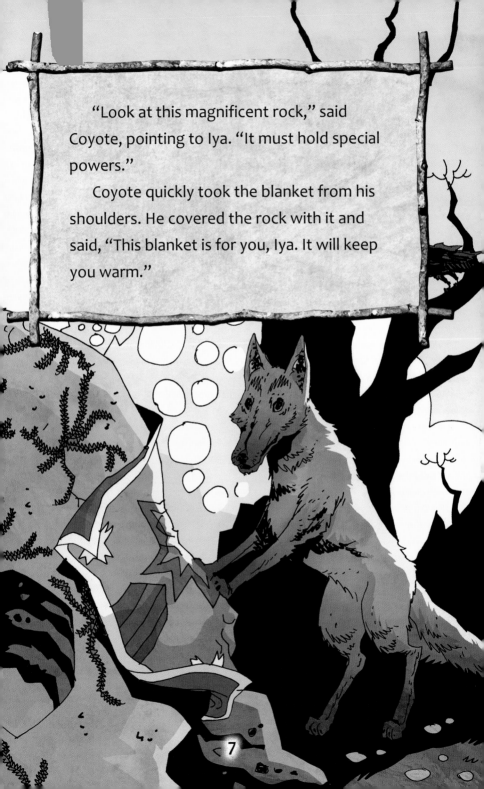

"Look at this magnificent rock," said Coyote, pointing to Iya. "It must hold special powers."

Coyote quickly took the blanket from his shoulders. He covered the rock with it and said, "This blanket is for you, Iya. It will keep you warm."

Iktome was surprised by his friend's kindness.

"What a nice thing to do," Iktome said.

Coyote simply shrugged. "It's a small gift," he said smiling. "Don't you think Iya looks nice in my blanket?"

"Yes," Iktome agreed. "And it's his now."

The two friends continued on their way. Soon, clouds rolled in, turning the sky black. It began to rain and hail.

Coyote and Iktome ran to a nearby cave to seek shelter from the storm. But the cave was not warm. It was cold and wet.

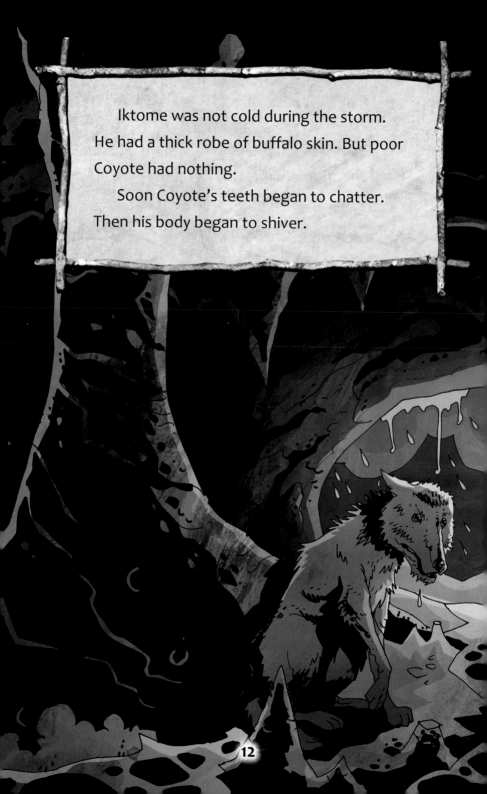

Iktome was not cold during the storm. He had a thick robe of buffalo skin. But poor Coyote had nothing.

Soon Coyote's teeth began to chatter. Then his body began to shiver.

"Would you go ask Iya to give back my blanket?" Coyote asked Iktome.

Coyote knew Iya could not truly need the blanket. How could a rock have any use for a blanket, after all?

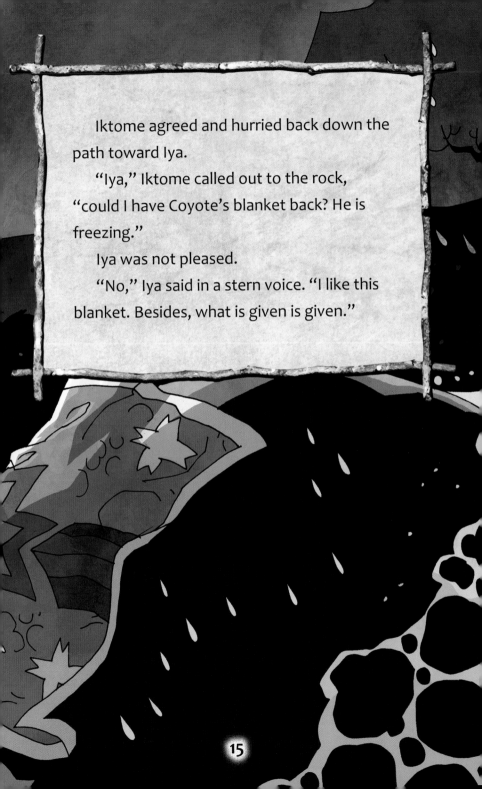

Iktome agreed and hurried back down the path toward Iya.

"Iya," Iktome called out to the rock, "could I have Coyote's blanket back? He is freezing."

Iya was not pleased.

"No," Iya said in a stern voice. "I like this blanket. Besides, what is given is given."

Iktome ran back to his friend and told him the bad news.

"Coyote, my friend," said Iktome, "I am so sorry, but I do not have your blanket."

"What happened?" asked Coyote.

"Iya is keeping the blanket," said Iktome.

Coyote was very angry.

"That rock never even paid me for that blanket!" Coyote shouted. "I will go ask for it myself."

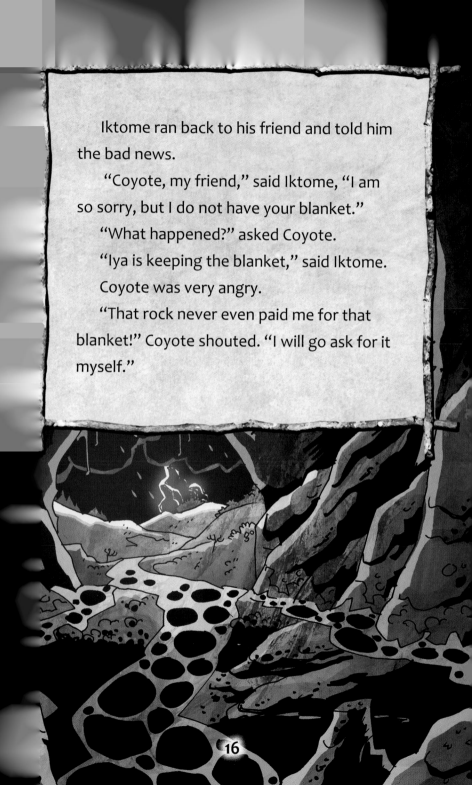

"Friend," Iktome said, "that rock has a lot of power. Perhaps you should just let him keep it."

Coyote did not listen to his friend. Instead, he set off down the trail.

"Look," Coyote said to the rock, "I need my blanket back."

"No," said Iya. "What is given is given."

"Look," Coyote said again to Iya, "I want my blanket back *right now*."

"No," said Iya. "What is given is given."

"You are not my friend," said Coyote. "A true friend would never let me freeze to death."

And with that, Coyote snatched the blanket off Iya and said, "This is over."

"This is not the end," said Iya.

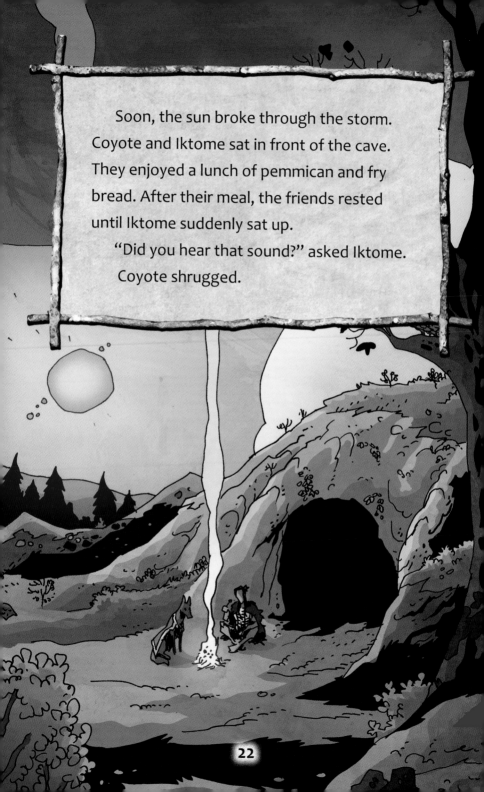

Soon, the sun broke through the storm. Coyote and Iktome sat in front of the cave. They enjoyed a lunch of pemmican and fry bread. After their meal, the friends rested until Iktome suddenly sat up.

"Did you hear that sound?" asked Iktome.

Coyote shrugged.

"I think it is thunder," said Iktome, looking around.

Coyote listened harder. "Yes, I hear it now," he said.

"Wait," said Iktome. "It is not thunder. It is Iya. He is coming for the blanket!"

The two friends jumped up and ran as fast as they could. But Iya came crashing right behind them.

Iktome pointed to a nearby river. "Let's swim across," he said. "Iya is so heavy he will sink!"

The two friends plunged into the river. But Iya rolled right over the waves after them.

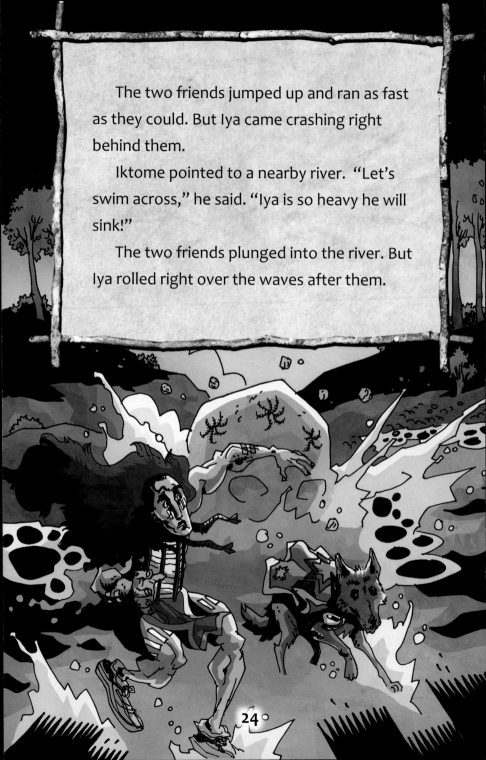

"Iktome," Coyote called to his friend, "let's hide in the thick forest where Iya can't get through to follow us."

The two friends ran into the deep woods. But Iya crushed the trees in his path as if they were twigs.

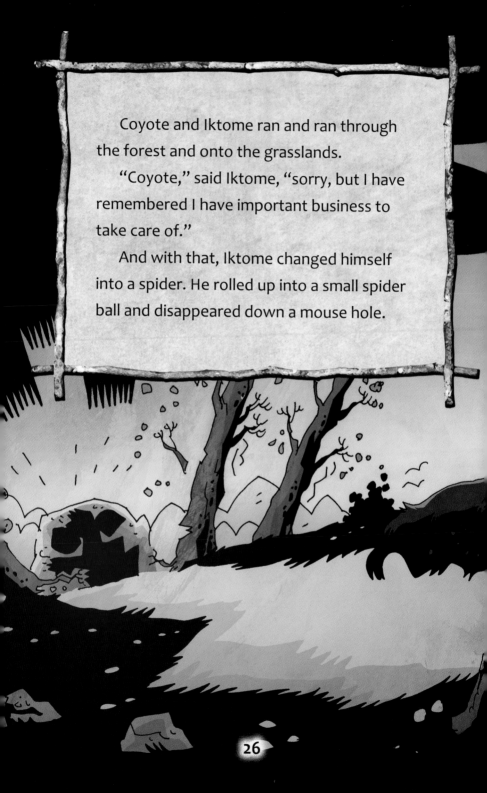

Coyote and Iktome ran and ran through the forest and onto the grasslands.

"Coyote," said Iktome, "sorry, but I have remembered I have important business to take care of."

And with that, Iktome changed himself into a spider. He rolled up into a small spider ball and disappeared down a mouse hole.

Poor Coyote was very tired. He tried to keep running but Iya caught up to him.

The rock rolled over Coyote, leaving him flatter than a blade of grass.

Iya snatched the blanket off Coyote and said, "What is given is given."

With that, Iya rolled back home.

Shortly after, a rancher found Coyote lying on the road.

"This would make a nice rug," the rancher said of flat Coyote, who appeared dead.

He picked up Coyote and took him home. He put Coyote in front of his fireplace.

But Coyote was not dead. Coyote could come back to life after he was killed. All night long, Coyote puffed and puffed to get back to his usual shape. By sunrise, he had succeeded.

In the morning, the rancher woke to find his rug missing.

"Your rug," said his wife, "just ran off."

So listen, friends, and learn from the lesson Iya taught Coyote. When you have something to give, you must give it forever.